Collins

THIS BOY

Pippa Goodhart

Illustrated by
Iva Sasheva

Chapter 1

Today had been a really bad day for Kerry. Coming into Year 9 as a new girl was never going to be easy. And this school was very different from her old one. All the kids had stared at her. Then the teacher had said, "I want you all to welcome Kerry into our class. Kerry, you can sit over there."

And Kerry had tripped over some boy's bag and fallen – crash! Hair all over the place. Face red. Bag spilled everywhere. Kids laughing and pointing. And they'd gone on laughing and pointing all day.

"That's it! I'm never going back there," thought Kerry, as she set off home after school.

Only "home" didn't feel like home any more.

Kerry and Mum had moved to a new house. The house was old and dark, and it made odd noises. As she walked slowly up the road, Kerry could see there were no lights on. Mum must still be at work. Kerry felt the front door key in her pocket, but she didn't take it out. "I'm not going in until Mum gets back," she thought.

There was a big stone cross just over the road from the house. It had a ledge around it that you could sit on. Kerry sat there as the empty street grew darker. She started to feel cold.

"Oh, I wish I could go back to how things were before!" she said out loud.

"So do I," said a voice behind her.

Kerry almost jumped out of her skin.

Chapter 2

It was a boy who had spoken, a tall skinny boy. He was wearing a type of army jacket with brass buttons. His hair was shorter than the boys' at school.

"Do you mind if I sit down?" said the boy.

"Yeah, sure," said Kerry. She could see that the boy's hands were shaking. His face was white.

"Are you OK?" said Kerry.

The boy closed his eyes for a moment and shook his head. "There are things that I need to do," he said. "But I can't do them."

"What sort of things?" asked Kerry. This boy was weird, but she didn't feel frightened of him.

"I have to tell Maggie that I'm sorry," said the boy. There was almost a sob in his voice.

"Who's Maggie?" said Kerry. "Your girlfriend?"

"My little sister," said the boy. "My brave little sister."

"Brave about what?" said Kerry, twisting around so that she could really look at the boy.

There was definitely something different about him, but she couldn't work out quite what it was.

The boy put his hands into his jacket pockets. "After her fifth birthday, Maggie had to start school."

"I had to start when I was four!" said Kerry, but the boy wasn't listening. He kept going with his story.

"Maggie didn't want to go to school. She was scared of the other children. She told me, 'I'll just have to pretend to be brave, won't I? Then maybe it will come true.' It made me feel very sad." The boy smiled gently.

"Maggie did try to be brave at school. And she told me that it worked. She made friends, and she even grew to like school in the end."

He paused. "I tried the same thing, you know. I pretended to be brave when I was in France."

"Have you been on holiday to France, then?" asked Kerry. She was about to laugh at the idea of having to be brave to go on holiday. But she saw the look on the boy's face, and stopped herself. "Did it work, pretending to be brave in France?"

"I suppose that it did, in a way," said the boy. Then he looked down and added, "But I just so wish that I had been brave before then, before I went to France."

"Why? What should you have been brave about?" asked Kerry.

Chapter 3

The boy took a deep breath, and began.

"Before I went to France, Father came home from one of his trips. He used to sell supplies to farms all over the place, you know. Anyway, he came home and he gave Maggie and me half-a-crown each."

"Half a what?" said Kerry.

"Half-a-crown," said the boy. Kerry looked at him, confused. "You know, money," he said. "He always gave me half-a-crown when he came home, but this was the first time he had given one to Maggie because she was so young.

Father told Maggie, 'Don't you lose that half-crown, girl!' And Maggie put the coin in her purse, and she didn't lose it.

But I did lose my half-crown. I have no idea where."

"That doesn't sound so bad," said Kerry.

"No, but you see, then Father wanted me to go with him to the fishing shop and buy a new rod he said was a good one. 'You can spend that half-crown on it,' he said. 'The one I gave you.'"

Then the boy said, "But of course I didn't have the half-crown any more. And, well, Father is not an easy sort of person once he's angry. I simply didn't dare tell him that I'd lost my coin."

He looked at Kerry. "So I stole Maggie's half-crown." He waved a hand. "I truly meant to pay it back as soon as I could. But …"

"France?" said Kerry.

The boy nodded. "France. I got my papers next day. I never had the chance to get the money for Maggie. And I didn't even tell her what I had done. She must have believed that she had lost that half-crown, and that it was her fault." The boy shrugged. "I was too much of a coward, you see."

"Yes, I do see. I can understand why you did it, though," said Kerry.

"I pretended to be brave in France, thinking that I would put it all right with Maggie when I got home to her. I should have written, I suppose.

But, well, I never have been any good with words. I had the money from my first pay all ready to give to Maggie. But then I never did leave France."

"You're home now," said Kerry. "Give it to her now!"

"It's too late," said the boy, sadly.

"Why?" asked Kerry.

"Because she's dead," said the boy.

"Oh, that's awful!" said Kerry. She wondered how and why Maggie had died, but she didn't want to pry. She touched the boy's hand. It felt very cold. "I'm a coward, too," she told him. "I don't even dare to go home. How pathetic is that?"

Just then, Kerry saw a light blink on in the house over the road. Mum must be home. She'd worry about where Kerry was.

"Actually, I'd better go home now," said Kerry.

"Do you have to? I wish …" began the boy. He stood up. "I suppose that I should go, too."

Kerry saw now that the boy had odd, dark bandages wrapped round the lower part of his legs. And he wore really old-style brown boots. As he stood up, he took something from his jacket pocket, and held it out to Kerry. It looked a bit like a silver medal.

"Here," he said. "I can't give it to Maggie, but at least I can give it to somebody who knows what I did. Somebody who knows that Maggie should have had it."

Kerry could see now that it wasn't a medal. It was a big coin.

The boy suddenly looked happier. "Please," he said, "what is your name?"

"Kerry Gordon," said Kerry.

"I'm Joe," said the boy. "Joe Brown." He shook her hand, but he didn't let it go again. He looked into Kerry's eyes. "Please, Kerry Gordon, would you mind … do you think that I might kiss your hand? I never did get to kiss a girl, you see."

Kerry laughed. "If you want!" she said. The boy lifted Kerry's hand to his lips. His touch was light and cold, but nice. He kissed Kerry's hand very softly. Then he smiled. "Do you know, I think that you have set me free, Miss Kerry Gordon!"

"Set you fr…?" began Kerry.

But the boy was gone, as suddenly as he had appeared.

Chapter 4

Kerry showed the half-crown coin to her mum. "That's old money," Mum told her. "They stopped using it back in the 1970s. It's a really early coin, too. Where did you get it from?"

"Just from this boy," said Kerry.

When Kerry went to school next day, she took the coin in her pocket. Feeling it there somehow made her feel braver.

"Hi!" said a girl. "Do you want me to show you the way to maths?"

"Yeah, please," said Kerry. The whole school day was okay like that. But Kerry was mostly thinking about the strange boy. She wondered if she would ever see him again.

Chapter 5

Kerry went back to the stone cross after school. A boy was standing there.

"Hello!" said Kerry.

"Hiya," said the boy. But he wasn't Joe.

"You're the new girl, aren't you?" he said. "I'm Jack."

"Oh!" said Kerry. She looked at the names carved onto the stone cross. Her fingers reached out and touched one of the names. The stone was old and worn, and the names weren't very clear.

Joseph Brown

"It says Joseph Brown," said Jack. "He was my Great-Great-Uncle Joe. Nan said he was only seventeen when he died in France in the First World War. I'm seventeen tomorrow and, well, it's too young to die."

Kerry felt so strange that she had to lean on the stone cross.

"Are you all right?" said Jack.

"I …," began Kerry. She took a deep breath. "I think I met Joe last night," she said. "I met him just here."

"Joe? You can't have!" said Jack. "Unless …"

There was a moment's silence between them. Then Kerry felt in her pocket. "But he was real enough to give me this." She held out the half-crown coin. "He said it was for his sister, Maggie."

"Nan said that her mum was called Maggie …" said Jack in wonder.

"Here. You have it," said Kerry. "I know he'd like you to have it." She held out the coin for Jack.

As Jack took the coin, he took hold of Kerry's hand as well. "Thank you," he said, and he held Kerry's hand just as Joe had done. But Jack's hand was warm. And this boy didn't disappear.

A note from the author

The First World War (1914–1918)

Over one hundred countries fought in the First World War. They fought all over the world, but mostly in Europe.

In France, the German and British soldiers dug trenches to defend themselves. The trenches were often just a hundred metres apart. The stalemate lasted for four years.

I imagined that Joe fought from a trench facing another trench full of German soldiers. Between them was "No Man's Land", bare of anything but barbed wire, bodies and mud.

Joe died in the Battle of the Somme. He was ordered to climb out of the trench and attack the Germans. The Germans had machine guns. Nearly twenty thousand soldiers in the British Army were killed on the first day.

By the end of the war, nearly nine million soldiers had been killed.

War memorials were put up in Britain to remember the dead.

Pippa Goodhart

Reader challenge

Word hunt

1. On page 5, find two words that describe the cross.
2. On page 22, find a word that means "flash".
3. On page 31, find a verb that means "cut".

Story sense

4. Why did Kerry not want to go home? (page 4)
5. What was Joe wearing? (page 6)
6. Why did Joe take Maggie's coin? (pages 15–16)
7. Why do you think Kerry felt braver with the coin in her pocket? (page 28)
8. How do you think Jack felt when Kerry gave him the coin? (page 35)

Your views

9 Did you know that Joe was a ghost? What clues were there in the story?

10 Did you feel sad for Joe? Give reasons.

Spell it

With a partner, look at these words and then cover them up.
- gave
- brave
- waved

Take it in turns for one of you to read the words aloud. The other person has to try and spell each word. Check your answers, then swap over.

Try it

With a partner, one of you takes on the role of Kerry. Pretend you are telling a friend the story of meeting Joe. Your friend must ask questions to find out what Joe was like.

William Collins's dream of knowledge for all began with the publication of his first book in 1819. A self-educated mill worker, he not only enriched millions of lives, but also founded a flourishing publishing house. Today, staying true to this spirit, Collins books are packed with inspiration, innovation and practical expertise. They place you at the centre of a world of possibility and give you exactly what you need to explore it.

Collins. Freedom to teach.

Published by Collins Education
An imprint of HarperCollins*Publishers*
77–85 Fulham Palace Road
Hammersmith
London
W6 8JB

Browse the complete Collins Education catalogue at **www.collinseducation.com**

Text by Pippa Goodhart © HarperCollins*Publishers* 2012
Illustrations by Iva Sasheva © HarperCollins*Publishers* 2012

Series consultants: Alan Gibbons and Natalie Packer

10 9 8 7 6 5 4 3 2 1
ISBN 978-0-00-746470-8

All rights reserved. No part of this publication may be reproduced, stored in a retrieval system, or transmitted in any form or by any means, electronic, mechanical, photocopying, recording or otherwise, without the prior written permission of the Publisher or a licence permitting restricted copying in the United Kingdom issued by the Copyright Licensing Agency Ltd, 90 Tottenham Court Road, London W1T 4LP.

British Library Cataloguing in Publication Data.
A catalogue record for this publication is available from the British Library.

Commissioned by Catherine Martin
Edited and project-managed by Sue Chapple
Illustration management by Tim Satterthwaite
Picture research and proofreading by Grace Glendinning
Design and typesetting by Jordan Publishing Design Limited
Cover design by Paul Manning

Acknowledgements

The publishers would like to thank the students and teachers of the following schools for their help in trialling the Read On series:

Southfields Academy, London; Queensbury School, Queensbury, Bradford; Langham C of E Primary School, Langham, Rutland; Ratton School, Eastbourne, East Sussex; Northfleet School for Girls, North Fleet, Kent; Westergate Community School, Chichester, West Sussex; Bottesford C of E Primary School, Bottesford, Nottinghamshire; Woodfield Academy, Redditch, Worcestershire;
St Richard's Catholic College, Bexhill, East Sussex

The publishers would like to thank the following for providing the pictures on these pages:

p36 National Media Museum, Bradford, West Yorkshire/flickr
p37 National Archives of the Netherlands/flickr